LAURA INGALLS WILDER

written and illustrated by
Alexandra Wallner

Holiday House / New York

Library of Congress Cataloging-in-Publication Data
Wallner, Alexandra.
Laura Ingalls Wilder / Alexandra Wallner. — 1st ed.
p.   cm.
Summary: A biography of the well-known author of "The Little House
on the Prairie," describing the pioneer experiences that provided
the basis for much of her writing.
ISBN 0-8234-1314-4 (hc)
1. Wilder, Laura Ingalls, 1867–1957—Biography—Juvenile
literature.   2. Women authors, American—20th century—Biography—
Juvenile literature.   3. Frontier and pioneer life—United States—
Juvenile literature.   4. Women pioneers—United States—Biography—
Juvenile literature.   5. Children's stories—Authorship—Juvenile
literature.   [1. Wilder, Laura Ingalls, 1867–1957.   2. Authors,
American.   3. Women—Biography.   4. Frontier and pioneer life.]
I. Title.
PS3545.I342Z93   1997   96-52917   CIP   AC
813′.52—dc21
[B]

To the spirit of those who have the courage to follow their dreams.
~A.W.

Laura Elizabeth Ingalls was born on February 7, 1867, near Pepin, Wisconsin, to Caroline and Charles Ingalls. Her sister Mary was two years older.

The family lived in a log cabin in the Big Woods. Wolves, bears, panthers, and foxes lived in the woods, too. But Laura and Mary felt safe with Ma and Pa.

In the evenings, they sat by the cozy fire. Ma read to them. Pa sang and played jolly tunes on his fiddle to make everyone laugh.

Ma raised vegetables, cooked, sewed, and kept house. Pa hunted game and grew crops for food.

Often Pa spoke about owning land where plowing would be easier. He dreamed of farming on the prairie.

In 1868 Pa sold the farm. The Ingalls packed their belongings in a covered wagon and headed West.

They traveled for many months. During the long journey Laura listened to Pa tell stories by the campfire.

When they came to Kansas at last, Laura saw land that looked like a sea of grass.

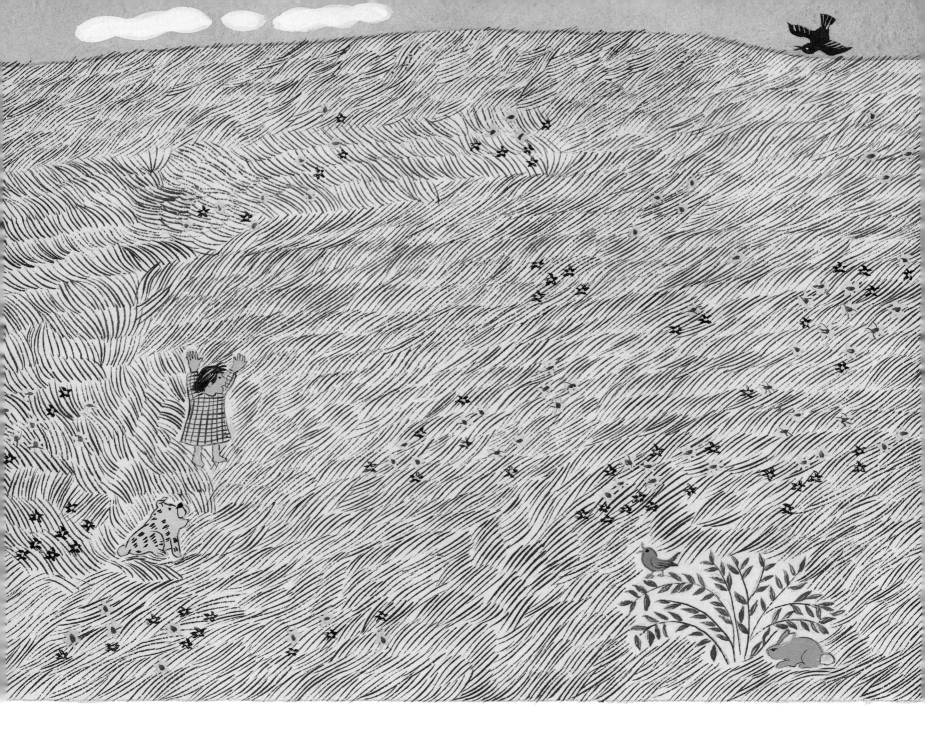

Pa built a cabin. In 1870 Laura's sister Carrie was born there.
Unknown to Pa, the cabin was on Osage Indian land and the Indians were angry.
At night Laura heard war cries that frightened her more than wolves howling.

Pa had no claim to the land and the family moved back to Wisconsin. But Pa missed the prairie, and in 1874 they moved near Walnut Grove, Minnesota.

Pa bought a dugout house made of sod and willow branches. Laura thought the house was strange, but Ma said it would be snug.

Mary helped Ma with chores and baby Carrie. Laura played on the prairie and
fished nearby in Plum Creek.

When a school was started in town, Laura was afraid
she couldn't play anymore. Soon, she discovered she liked
school, especially reading and writing.

Pa expected to make a lot of money from his wheat crop, so he built a real house. It had yellow pine boards, glass windows, and china doorknobs. Laura had never seen such a fine house.

But during the summer, grasshoppers invaded the prairie and ate the wheat. The next summer, the grasshoppers came again. Pa had no wheat to sell. The family had to leave the fine house.

More trouble followed. Laura's baby brother Freddie died soon after he was born. Because Pa couldn't find work, the family had to move many times. Everyone was sad, but when Pa played his fiddle in the evenings, its sweet melodies comforted them. They were also cheered by the birth of Laura's sister Grace in 1877.

Then the family moved back to Walnut Grove where Pa worked at odd jobs.

One winter Mary caught a fever and lost her eyesight. From then on, Laura became
Mary's eyes. When they walked on the prairie, Laura described the changing seasons,
the sunsets, and everything she saw to Mary. Laura was learning to make pictures
with words.

In 1879 Pa found a job in Silver Lake, Dakota Territory, working in a store for the railroad. When the railroad construction camp closed for the winter, he became its watchman.

The family lived in the surveyor's house. During the long winter nights, Pa told stories. Laura never tired of Pa's wonderful stories.

Laura read aloud from books and newspapers, always saving part of the story for the next night. Everyone wanted to know what happened next.

In the spring, the Ingalls moved to De Smet, a new town in Dakota Territory. Pa no longer dreamed of farming on the prairie, and he promised Ma they would not have to move again.

Laura was happy living near school. Even so, school was often closed because of deep snow, and Laura studied at home. She read her family's books over and over and borrowed others. She wrote poems in little books she made herself.

In the winter of 1880, blizzard after blizzard swept across the prairie. The town was running out of food. Two young men, Almanzo Wilder and Cap Garland, made a dangerous trip in sleighs across the frozen prairie to get wheat from a farmer who had a big supply. They kept the townsfolk from starving. Laura thought Almanzo was a real hero.

Because she was a good student, Laura was asked to teach at a prairie school. She was lonely away from her family. One Friday, Almanzo surprised her by coming in a sleigh to take her home. She stayed with her family all weekend, then Almanzo took her back on Sunday. He did the same every weekend.

Laura taught at two more prairie schools. But like most frontier girls, she did not graduate from high school. She loved Almanzo, whom she called Manly, and married him in 1885.

A year later, their daughter was born. Laura named her Rose after the bright pink flowers that bloomed on the prairie. Laura and Manly were happy.

Soon though, the Wilders suffered hard times. Hail, drought, and fierce windstorms ruined their wheat crops and made them poor. Their baby son died soon after he was born. A serious illness left Manly weak.

To help him recover, Laura and Manly moved to Minnesota with his family, then to Florida, where it was warm.

They returned to De Smet, but life on the prairie was too harsh. In 1894 they decided to try farming in the milder climate of the Ozark Mountains. They traveled to Missouri, where they found lush fields and tree-covered mountains.

Laura kept a notebook about the journey. A week before reaching Mansfield, Missouri, she sent a letter describing her trip to a newspaper in De Smet. It was published and Laura proudly wrote in the margin, "First I ever had published."

With a hundred dollars Laura had earned from sewing, she and Manly made a down payment on land near Mansfield she called "Rocky Ridge Farm."

In the gentler climate of the Ozarks, Laura raised chickens and grew fruit trees. Soon the farm prospered. Laura would not move again.

Once the farm was well established, Laura decided to share her knowledge about farming. In 1911 she started writing articles for a paper, the *Missouri Ruralist*, and soon had a column called "As a Farm Woman Thinks."

A few years later, Rose, who was now a well-known writer, urged her mother to write for national magazines. Laura took her advice and did.

But Laura wanted to do more than that. She wanted to write about her life as a pioneer girl. Her memories and Pa's stories "... were too good to be altogether lost." She wanted "to do some writing that will count."

She wrote and revised a story called "Pioneer Girl" many times. Finally a book company wanted to publish it, if she rewrote it for children. She did.

In 1932, when Laura was sixty-five, her first book *Little House in the Big Woods* was published.

Readers loved it. They wanted to know what happened next. Laura wrote seven more books about her family. She was pleased that many people enjoyed her stories. Laura was as good at writing stories as Pa had been at telling them.

In 1949 Manly died at the age of ninety-two.

Although Laura was lonely without him, she kept busy answering fan letters and seeing visitors.

Reflecting about her hard, but rewarding life, she wrote, "It is still best to be honest and truthful; to make the most of what we have; to be happy with simple pleasures and to be cheerful and have courage when things go wrong."

Laura died on February 10, 1957, three days after her ninetieth birthday.

Laura once said she had written her stories because, "I wanted the children now to understand more about the beginnings of things, to know what is behind the things they see—what it is that made America as they know it."

AUTHOR'S NOTE

The LITTLE HOUSE books are:

Little House in the Big Woods 1932
Farmer Boy 1933
Little House on the Prairie 1935
On the Banks of Plum Creek 1937*
By the Shores of Silver Lake 1939*
The Long Winter 1940*
Little Town on the Prairie 1941*
These Happy Golden Years 1943*
The First Four Years 1971

Laura wrote eight *Little House* books. The ninth book, *The First Four Years*, was published in 1971 from notes Laura had kept. The books have been published in more than forty different languages.

Books marked with a * have been named Newbery Honor Books.

In 1954 the American Library Association created the Laura Ingalls Wilder Award to honor an author or illustrator whose books have made a substantial and lasting contribution to literature for children. Laura received the first award.